The Boy and the Whale

A Sea World Edition™

Published by

THIRD STORY BOOKS™
955 Connecticut Avenue, Suite 1302
Bridgeport, Connecticut 06607

ISBN 1-884506-15-1

Distributed to the trade by
Andrews & McMeel
4900 Main Street
Kansas City, Missouri 64112

Library of Congress Catalog Card Number: 94-60731

Book design by Joanna Wiebe and Ron Jaffe

DEDICATIONS

I dedicate this book to the Lopez family, with special dedication to my nephew Michael
P. Lopez, and my wife Rosa. Also, special thanks to my friends at Third Story Books.
Paul J. Lopez

For Mark, for Yolie, and for John-Mark Browne.
Eric Metaxas

Printed in Hong Kong

1 2 3 4 5 6 7 8 9 10
FIRST EDITION

The Boy and the Whale

A CHRISTMAS FAIRY TALE

By Eric Metaxas

Illustrated by Paul Lopez

THIRD STORY BOOKS

*O*nce upon a time there was a boy in a lighthouse. His father and mother lived there with him, for his father was the lighthouse keeper, just as his father had been before him. Now this particular lighthouse was on a rather small, rocky island, some miles out to sea. And because the boy's mother and father were generally consumed with the great details and extraordinary responsibilities of running the lighthouse – lest any errant ship should come to be wrecked on their rocky shore – the boy often felt very much as though he lived alone, as though he were the only soul on a small planet surrounded by an endless universe of eternal blue.

So the boy spent hours and hours wishing that he had someone – a friend – with whom he might enjoy the long and salty and windy days. He so wanted someone to talk to and to play with. But most of the time the boy put these thoughts out of his mind and occupied himself in doing more practical things like looking for lobsters and mussels, which he proudly brought home to his mother for supper.

When the boy was not making himself useful in any outward way he would often just sit on a barnacled rock and watch the ocean heave and swell as it went he knew not where, for it seemed to be going somewhere and nowhere and everywhere all at once. He loved the sea in all of its guises: he loved it when it was choppy and agitated; and he loved it when there were great powerful swells that seemed to have come from the other side of the world; and he loved it when it was so extraordinarily calm that it seemed one could easily step out upon its pure, glassy surface and walk all the way to the horizon.

And the boy sometimes wondered what it was like *below* the changing surface, where the fish and other animals lived, and where it was always the same, quiet and calm, untouched by the weather in the fickle world above. He thought of the watery realm below the surface as a secret world, and sometimes as he sat there he would imagine that he could go down there and swim among the sea creatures, just as though he were one of them, and he thought, *then I wouldn't be lonely at all, for there are so very many of them down there to play with.*

He loved all of the creatures that swam about in the depths of the waters. But of all the myriad animals that dwelt there the boy loved best the great whales that roamed the deepest waters of the world's oceans and which would sometimes surface – quite suddenly – in his little part of the world to blow warm vapor into the atmosphere. The boy knew that they were mammals, and that they breathed with lungs, just as he did, not with gills. And it was for this reason, and for the reason that they were sometimes above the water and sometimes below it, that they held for him a kind of unique place between the two worlds, the world of the sea and the world of the men. It was as though the great whales were messengers between the two worlds.

Now, the boy knew that there were various types of whales, but the type he most thought of was called *Orcinus orca,* or what his father called a grampus, or a killer whale. He didn't see them often, but every once in a great while, when he was occupied collecting mussels, or lobsters among the rocks, he would catch sight of one breaking the water near him and it would take his breath away. *What must it be like to touch one of them,* he wondered. They were the most magnificent creatures he could imagine. Whenever he laid eyes on one it was as though time itself stopped, as though eternity had poked its head above the waters.

One day while he was watching the water's smooth surface and thinking of nothing in particular, a strange idea seemed to swim from beyond the horizon right into his head. He thought: *If I could have a friend – a true friend – I would want it to be a whale!* He knew that it would be impossible, but if he was going to wish he might as well wish a great wish, and what wish could be greater than that?

But then he realized that Christmas was coming! How the boy loved Christmas. Perhaps his father would make him a toy whale out of wood for Christmas! They could paint it together, black and white, just like the whales the boy so loved. And he might talk to it and make of it an imaginary friend, which could sometimes be almost as good as a real live friend. *Yes,* he thought, *that's what I want for Christmas.* And he thought of it over and over... *a whale for Christmas, a whale for Christmas, I want a whale for Christmas...* And the more he mumbled this to himself the more real it seemed, as though it wasn't just an idle fancy, but something actual that he would soon possess.

In the days that followed – for Christmas was fast approaching – the boy began to drop hints here and there around his parents. But for some reason they never seemed to be paying much attention when he was making a comment. Perhaps it was already too late, he thought. It seemed as if they had already bought the presents they were going to buy, for people who live on an island miles and miles out to sea have never had the luxury of shopping at the last minute. The prospects for his whale didn't look very promising.

But that very night, when saying his prayers, the boy looked out his window and into the vast heavens where the stars were shimmering and he said, "Oh God, *please* let me have a whale for Christmas!" When he prayed this he imagined the beautifully carved wooden whale gleaming with a new, shiny coat of black and white paint, as beautiful as a real, live whale. And his longing for it – and for the companionship it would provide, whether imaginary or not – was so strong, that for a moment it seemed to the boy not to be a wooden whale at all, but a real one, which is how all of the truest imaginary friends always seem. And with that done the boy crawled into bed and fell fast asleep.

*N*ow, the truth of the matter is that the purity of the boy's request was such that something quite magnificent happened. You see, the prayer traveled as fast as light through the clouds in the sky (prayers do travel, you know) and on through the thinning atmosphere, up and up and up, until it at last found its way into the very heart of heaven itself. And when God saw it he was so touched by it – for it was one of the purest prayers he had ever seen – that he did something he ordinarily doesn't do. He shared the boy's request with a shining star.

And as soon as the star heard it, it gave a shiver of delight (you may have noticed it twinkling if you were looking up at the sky that night). And so that star told another star who told another and another and another until the whole brilliant canopy of heaven was aflutter with the poignant news of the boy's request.

It would not be an untruth to tell you that astronomers the world over scratched their heads that night in wonderment at such a terrific twinkling of stars. None of them had ever seen anything like it. "Perhaps it is a disturbance in our own atmosphere due to the volcanic ash in the jet stream," they exclaimed, but of course you know that had nothing to do with it.

And then a young star, off alone in his own quadrant of the sky, heard about it. He was one of the last ones to hear about it, for he lived far off from the other stars. But when he heard the story of the boy's loneliness and desire for companionship he was so moved – for he was often quite lonely himself, living out there at the edge of the sky – that he volunteered to take the message to earth himself so that something could be done. And so he did. In an explosion of love the star burst from his station in the heavens and fell to the earth – falling and falling and falling, in a great, blazing shower of light.

Somewhere, far out in the ocean, on a coral reef, there was a gathering of sea stars that night. And as he plummeted toward the earth the star saw them and because all he had ever known were stars he landed in the water near them. And there in the water, with his last breath, he told the sea stars what the stars in heaven had learned: "There is a lighthouse," he said. "And on the island where the lighthouse is there is a little boy whose only wish is that he would have a whale as a friend for Christmas. Please help him, for he is lonely, and it is a terrible thing to be lonely." And with that the last rays of his brilliant light melted into the December seas.

Now, one of the sea stars who heard this ached to do something about it. So he did the only thing he could do: he told a sandworm. And the sandworm told a flounder, who told a sea robin, who told his closest friend – who happened to be an eel – and the eel told his brothers, who in a group traveled to the lair of a grouper and, all talking at once, relayed the message to him. And the grouper, when it was time for dinner, swam up several hundred feet to where a school of mackerel were and told the whole school about the boy who was looking for the whale. The school talked among themselves excitedly and told an old sea turtle, who in turn told an ancient crab. And he, of course, told a mossy old lobster, who was nearly as old as the ocean itself, and the lobster told it to a clam, who may have been older than the ocean, and the clam kept it to himself, as clams are wont to do.

But that's only at low tide, when clams are susceptible to predators, you understand. When the tide rises, as it always has, clams are every bit as talkative as anyone. In fact, more talkative, for they have to say everything they want to say while the tide is still high. And so, when the tide finally rose the clam opened up and told a pilot whale. And the pilot whale had recently made the acquaintance of a gray whale, whom he told, and in a short time the message had traveled throughout the entire world of whaledom, until, as last, it was communicated to a certain pod of killer whales, among whom lived one very special whale.

When this whale heard about the boy who longed for a friend and who loved whales, his heart was deeply touched and, powerless to do anything else, he began the long, long journey toward a certain island, where stood a certain lighthouse, where lived a certain boy, somewhere beyond the curved blue horizon.

When it was only two days until Christmas the boy in the lighthouse wondered if his prayer would be answered. *A whale for Christmas!* he thought, *a whale for Christmas!* He'd watched his mother baking all that week, the way she did every Christmas, and his anticipation grew with every scent he caught of cinnamon, or gingerbread spice, that wafted from the kitchen window down to the rocks where he sat. How glorious it would be to have a friend! The small fact that this friend was to be made of wood did not discourage the boy for, as you know, one's imagination can make up for a host of shortcomings.

On Christmas Eve the boy helped decorate their Christmas tree, which they kept for all twelve days of Christmas every year, as they did all their Christmas decorations. The boy used some of the favorite shells he'd collected. There was every kind imaginable: there were whelks and there were jingle shells and moon shells and limpets and there were blue mussel shells and scallop shells and quahog shells and there were even periwinkles. And for the very top of the tree – for its crown, his mother called it – the boy had found a sea star! But when he located it in the box of ornaments he saw that it had been broken. And so, the top of the tree, at least for this Christmas, would wear no crown.

After the tree was decorated they ate dinner together. Christmas Eve dinner was always the boy's favorite meal of the year, and afterward they would open their presents. The boy's eyes scanned the wrapped gifts around the tree. But he didn't see anything that looked like it might be a wooden whale. And indeed, once he'd unwrapped his gifts, he saw that there was no whale among them. The boy was devastated. And although his other presents were what he had wanted before he had gotten to thinking about the whale (a pair of woolen mittens and a drum and a set of tin soldiers) he found it difficult to appear enthusiastic. This, coupled with the fact that he went to bed early, *without* having to be told, made his parents think that he must be catching a cold.

Once the boy was in bed he could think of nothing else but the whale he had hoped for and wished for and prayed for. Had he done something wrong? He looked outside his window and saw that a gentle snow had begun to fall. It made him feel a little better to see that it was snowing on Christmas Eve. At least he would have a white Christmas, he thought, and perhaps he might even make a snowman and then the snowman could be his imaginary friend. At least until it melted. But a friend for a short period of time was better than no friend at all, which is a great truth acknowledged by all the poets and philosophers of the universe. So it was on this thought that the boy's mind dissolved into its own soothing ocean of sleep.

When Christmas morning finally came the boy saw that the snow had stopped, but it had left a layer of white powder several inches thick, transforming his island into even more of a glistening, arctic world. There seemed to be enough snow to build a snowman, and the boy decided he would do just that, and perhaps after that he would come inside and play with his new tin soldiers. He put on two pair of woolen socks and his rubber Wellington boots and a sweater and his oilskin jacket and his new mittens and he went downstairs, past the starless tree, and out the door and down the path to the water.

He stood on his favorite rock and looked out toward the horizon. How much he wanted a friend! He began rolling a snowball larger and larger for the base of his snowman. But his heart was not in it. How could he become friends with a snowman when he'd already become friends with the whale in his imagination? Even if the wooden whale had not materialized under the Christmas tree, it existed in his mind and imagination. It existed in his heart, in the place where all things really existed.

The boy left off rolling the large snowball and sighed. And again, for no reason he knew of, he looked out over the water. And there, some yards out, the boy saw a shiny black and white form breast the surface of the water and exhale a warm plume of vapor into the cold Christmas air. Was it possible? Was the boy dreaming? And then it swam toward him – toward *him* – as real as the whale that had lived in his imagination all these weeks.

The boy bent down. And the whale swam right up to him! It seemed almost to know him somehow. And he seemed to know *it*. It was the very whale he had imagined. "Oh, I knew you would come!" the boy cried. "I knew you would come!" The boy heard his father's fiddle music – for his father always played his fiddle on Christmas morning. And as the music danced through the air the boy knew that this was not a dream and that the whale had indeed come – it had come to him – a whale for Christmas, just as he'd hoped. And he knew that he would not be alone anymore, at least for a little while, just for a little while. He was as happy as it was possible to be. Then the boy recalled a bedtime story his father had once told him about a certain killer whale named Shamu. It gave him a grand idea. "I will call you Shamu," he cried out to the whale. "Shamu!" Tears welled up in his eyes and, unable to contain his happiness, he danced from rock to rock along the shoreline, kicking the white snow as he did, and the whale swam alongside him.

And so the boy at last had a friend. It was all that he had ever dreamt of, a whale for Christmas! A whale for Christmas! All morning he and Shamu played together along the snowy shore, the boy running and Shamu leaping into the air with delight. After lunch the boy rowed out from the island in his little rowboat. Shamu would disappear under the waves and then, suddenly, rise up and bump the boat with his nose playfully, and the boy would scream with laughter. It was *more* than he had ever dreamt.

So it went. The next morning, as soon as the sun's rays came into his room, the boy got dressed and ran down the path to the rocks to look for his new friend. "Shamu! Shamu!" he cried, wondering whether his memories of the previous day had been a dream, but then the whale appeared and their second day together began. The second day of Christmas! It was twice as much fun as the first had been and the boy thought he would burst with happiness. He somehow knew in the back of his mind that Shamu would have to go back to the place he had come from when the twelve days of Christmas were over, but that still seemed so very far away, and there was so much to do in the meantime.

*A*nd so the days passed, each one filled with the joys of friendship which the boy had always longed for. Sometimes, to the boy's unspeakable delight, Shamu would bring him things from deep under the sea, or breach the water several times, each breach seeming to carry him higher than the time before. Each day brought a new adventure.

One day while they were in a cove on the far side of the island, they came suddenly upon a group of killer whales. Although the boy knew that Shamu loved him with all his heart, and he loved Shamu, he nevertheless sensed that his time with the big whale would soon come to an end. And then the boy remembered that tomorrow was the twelfth day of Christmas! But it couldn't be! How quickly time had passed! It didn't seem possible.

That night as he lay in bed the boy could not sleep. He knew that tomorrow might be his last day with Shamu . But the boy's sadness at the thought of losing his dear friend was unimaginable. Twelve days was so short! Then he became angry: *I didn't ask for a real whale!* he thought. *I could have had a wooden whale forever! Then this would have never happened!* But he knew in his heart that his time with Shamu, however brief, was worth more than an eternity of wooden whales. There was nothing more to say.

In the morning, when Shamu came up to him he leaned over and touched Shamu's nose tenderly. He spoke with great resolve. "You know I love you, and that I care more about you than I do myself. Perhaps you can come visit me again next Christmas." Shamu saw that there were tears in the boy's eyes, and the thought of leaving the boy filled him with sadness.

And then something quite inconceivable and unprecedented took place. It was as if suddenly the boy had stepped into another world, as though he had passed through a mirror. For he realized that he suddenly knew Shamu's every thought, and Shamu knew his. And Shamu told him that they would go on one last trip together before his friend returned to the place from which he had come.

Then it happened: in the next moment the boy found himself on Shamu's back, riding with him into the water. Something magical truly had happened, and in another moment something yet more amazing took place, for before the boy knew it, he and the whale were both under the water, on the other side, below the shifting surface, below the wind and the waves, traveling together, gliding and soaring like aquatic angels, in the depths of the blue sea.

The boy could not comprehend all of the marvels he saw. As they swam along they were greeted by great schools of fish. Each of the fish that passed them seemed to know who he was, as though they'd heard of him and spoken of him among themselves long ago. When he and Shamu passed over a vast oyster bed, casting a great shadow as they did, the oysters each snapped a greeting to him in turn. Shamu dove deeper and the boy saw great sharks swimming about in their dull, predatory way, but he knew that he was safe on Shamu's back. He saw sea horses and bluefish and striped bass and sea robins, and he saw graceful rays flitting across the sandy bottom like windswept leaves.

They traveled on and on through the blue depths and the boy's heart leapt at all that his eyes took in. A sea turtle swam near them, so close that the boy touched its back, and a beautiful blue marlin followed it, piercing the water as he went. And then, beyond them as they swam, the boy in wonder beheld a pair of eels undulating through the water like music.

I'm in a dream, the boy thought, *I'm inside a dream*. But he knew that he wasn't dreaming. Weren't his memories of the time when he was lonely and had no one to play with the dream? Had that time ever really existed? It seemed that he and the whale had been together here under the water forever, and it was the other world and his life above the water that were fragments of a sad and distant dream that he had dreamed long, long ago.

They continued on through the endless water, passing towering underwater cliffs that teemed with sea life. They swam past a large, sunken ship lying in its watery grave on the sandy bottom. It had probably made its last voyage more than a hundred years before.

Soon the boy saw sea creatures that he did not recognize from any of his books, and he knew they were in another part of the ocean from where they had started. And at last, after traveling a long, long time they came to a great coral reef that seemed to stretch in every direction. The boy saw that there were sea stars on it everywhere, as far as the eye could see. And here Shamu stopped.

The boy saw that near the thousands of sea stars, alone and off by itself, there lay a single sea star. It did not have the brilliant color of the other sea stars, and when the boy saw it lying there, lifeless and forlorn, his heart broke. Now, although the boy did not know it, this sea star had once been a star in the night sky – for it was none other than the very star that had, out of its love for the boy, left heaven and come to earth. The boy was so touched by it, lying alone there, that he could not help himself. He reached out and picked up the sea star and looked at it. "May he come home with me and be my friend?" the boy asked Shamu. Shamu nodded. And so the boy took the sea star and, climbing back onto Shamu, put it in his pocket. Then they began the long journey home.

At last they came to the rock where they had first met and there they said their tear-filled good-byes. Perhaps they would meet again next Christmas. The boy hugged Shamu as hard as he could. It broke his heart to leave his friend whom he loved more than anything in the world, but he knew that he must. And so he turned away and walked toward the lighthouse.

When he got inside he saw that the Christmas tree was still up, for today was, after all, the twelfth and last day of Christmas. And still the tree had no crown. It seemed so incomplete. Then the boy remembered something. He reached into his pocket. It was still there! The sea star! He took it out and looked at it. It no longer looked lifeless and forlorn. Not in the least, for a strange thing had taken place since he put it in his pocket, and it now seemed filled with life.

It was more beautiful than he could have imagined. There was a certain radiance to it that he could not comprehend, as though his sea star glowed with the very light of heaven itself. The boy's heart leapt. He climbed onto a chair and put the sea star on the top or the tree and smiled.

And now as he beheld it, the boy's heart was filled with its light, and he knew he would never be lonely again.

$\mathcal{E}$ric $\mathcal{M}$etaxas

Eric is the former editorial director of *Rabbit Ears Productions*, and the renowned author of more than twenty children's books and videos. His work has won several *Parents Choice Awards* for outstanding children's videos.

$\mathcal{P}$aul $\mathcal{L}$opez

Paul is perhaps best known for his fabulous and realistic marine life paintings. His work has been featured in many books, as well as in educational art posters for Sea World of California and Florida.